Joanne was born and raised in Bradford, West Yorkshire. She feels lucky enough to have been given a chance to write her first children book at the good old age of 44!

"Let our children be safe and happy... Let them escape to a different place... Let them dream..."

i

TALES FROM
BLUEBELL FARM

JOANNE CLARKE

AUSTIN MACAULEY PUBLISHERS™
LONDON • CAMBRIDGE • NEW YORK • SHARJAH

Copyright © Joanne Clarke (2021)

A CIP catalogue record for this title is available from the British Library.

ISBN 9781528987608 (Paperback)
ISBN 9781528987615 (ePub e-book)

www.austinmacauley.com

First Published (2021)
Austin Macauley Publishers Ltd
25 Canada Square
Canary Wharf
London
E14 5LQ

For my beautiful boy, Uri.

Thanks to my beautiful son, Uri. To my mum, who is always there when I can't even make it out of the house! And to everyone at Austin Macauley for believing in me and giving me a chance.

Welcome…to Bluebell farm, I'm Monsieur Bertie and Im used to taking charge of things around here. I'm a natural leader, a runner—a very fast runner, that's because I'm a runner bean! I'm tall and slim, very strong and lean; did I mention how fast I am…? But enough about me, let me introduce you to all of the others that live here on the farm.

Agnes Moriarty:
Is the lady who owns and runs Bluebell farm; she isn't as young as she once was, so she's unable to do the manual work in the gardens, such as the veggie patch. She spends most of her days in with the flowers, picking and arranging them nicely to sell in the shop which is joined onto the old farmhouse. That's why Miss Agatha and Lady Lilliana think they're the best and most important because Agnes spends most of her time with them.

Lady Lilliana:
Is the most beautiful Lily you've ever seen, so elegant and slender; she has such a delicate manner—not like Agatha who can be rather abrupt.

Miss Agatha:
Is a big pink Geranium, a nice full bloom, but nothing special, although she most definitely thinks so! She thinks that because she was one of the first ones here on the farm, just like myself 25 years ago!

Percival Pea:
We have little Percival pea. Who I must say is a cheery one, a little rascal! Trying to get away with whatever he can; all the time rolling between different patches. He spends most of his time down at Butterfly farm. The lady who looks after them, 'FLEUR', is such a gentle soul; she always smells of beautiful perfume and he loves spending his time around her …

Doris and Delilah:
Two of the most exquisite butterflies you have ever laid eyes on. They move and fly around so gracefully; it's wonderful to be able to watch them and the most beautiful colours they have on their wings, that sparkle and glisten in the sunshine.

Old Bramble:
Back on the veggie patch, Old Bramble tends to the upkeep, with my help of course! And that too of 'PIPPA', his faithful dog, who also enjoys pulling up a carrot or two!

Bizzie, Bossy and Flossy:
All line up on the berry patch. I don't know exactly what kind of berries they are; they all have different colours and sometimes they can even change in the sun. Bizzie is green with bobbly bits, Bossy is red and Flossy is a lovely deep purple. They are always gossiping and twittering, anytime you need to know anything, go and ask these three!
"Oh, I nearly forgot..."

Hip and Hop:
Two fluffy bunnies, with the most magnificent, round, soft full tails! They're so mischievous, here, there and everywhere. Just like Pippa, they're partial to a carrot or two or three or four...
That's about it really...there's not a lot of us, but we all live happily alongside one another. We always have things going on, maybe a fate or celebration day and also selling days, where people come to buy and sell their produce. Two of our more regular visitors are 'Miss Polly and Miss Dolly'; twin girls. Miss Agnes is their great aunt and they come and spend the holidays with us.
So...shall we get started on one of the tales from Bluebell farm?

Whatever Happened to Percival?

The sun rose early and you could feel the heat to its glorious rays, that was good because we were having a large vegetable market on the big lawn. You could hear a nearby cock—a—doodle—doing to wake everybody up. Everyone was busy, busy, busy putting up stalls and tables; potatoes, cabbage, cauliflowers, turnips, carrots, runner beans, peapods, lettuce, spring onions and radish. Pears and apples from the fruit trees and every type of berry you could think of.

Fleur brought lots and lots of tomatoes which she grows inside where the butterflies are kept. Doris and Delilah were practising a little dance routine which was to open the beginning of the market and of course little Percival sat amazed watching Fleur's every move!

Of course, Miss Agatha and Lady Lilliana had their own large stall. Showing off Agnes Moriarty's beautiful blooms.

Everything had to be the best; Miss Agatha had to be the best! The neighbouring farms bring and sell their goods, such as cheese, pies and home baked goodies.

It was so busy and as people started to arrive. I didn't want little Percival to get squashed. So, told him to go and play up in the meadow with Hip+Hop who were busy amusing themselves, jumping over the stream which ran alongside the meadow and veggie patches.

The butterfly dance went off beautifully and Fleur was extremely proud of Doris and Delilah. It was a lovely day, everyone was happy, a lot of happy customers and sellers—there wasn't hardly anything left at the end of the day; it had been a great success.

Slowly the people drifted away and the stalls were taken down. By the time we had eaten, the sun was starting to set and Hip+Hop were playing on the lawn. "Where's Percival?" I asked. Both sets of ears pricked up and they looked startled and both scurried off. Where is he? I thought; he was always around, close by. At bedtime I went back up to the vegetable patch, but still no sign of Percival!

The night passed quickly without a wink of sleep, then as the sun came up, a quick tap on the door—when I opened Mrs Bramble—Old Bramble's wife stood there with Hip+ Hop!

"These 2 have something to tell you Monsieur Bertie." "Wwwe...we are sorry for thumping off so quickly yesterday, but we were scared because of what happened—we were playing paper boats on the stream when Percival jumped in!

and he was carried all the way down, until we couldn't see him anymore!"
I was very angry and scowled. Why had they not told me this yesterday?
Mrs Bramble said they were so sorry and had felt so bad they decided that they had to tell her.
Of course, I ran, ran and ran all the way at the side of the stream to see where Percival had ended up, but nothing. I wanted to cry, I sat down to rest my legs and must have dozed off because I was so tired.

I was awakened by all the fluttering around me, lots of butterflies then Doris and Delilah appeared—and guess who was with them? Yes—Percival! Delilah held him so tight. "I thought I had lost you, my sweet little Percival."

As soon as the butterflies had heard, they all went in search of the little Fella, and as I had been running at one side of the stream, he was slowly trying to roll up the other!

Oh...I was so happy, that I'd found him. I wasn't going to let him out of my sight again.

"Can we go home now, I'm hungry."

Miss Polly and Miss Dolly
Make a Scarecrow

It was just the very start of the summer holidays and Miss Polly and Miss Dolly were coming to stay. I sometimes think they get in the way and poke their noses into things they shouldn't; that's why, I nicknamed them 'the nosey–pokes'.
Everyone else seemed to love them, probably because of the fact that all they wanted to do was play and play all day long.

One day as we were all sat on the lawn having a picnic, Ms Agnes came out and said, "The farm had done so well at the market fair. There was enough money to make a new scarecrow. As the old one wasn't of much use anymore. It was dropping to pieces; the big crows from Applemeres farm had picked it to bits! So much for scaring off the birds! Oh, what a lovely idea, a new project."

Bluebell, a rusty coloured cow used to live next door at Robins farm;

she had been there for quite a while, but in recent months had been sneaking through the hedge and into the high meadow. I think she likes it here better and there was no point on taking her back because the very next day she'd be here again! So, she stayed with us. Mr Robin had given her the name Bluebell because she used to play amongst them when she was a calf.

She said she'd be able to fetch a bale of straw from the barn at Robins farm and roll it over the hedge.

Miss Polly and Miss Dolly jumped in excitement; that would be wonderful. It would do just fine for the stuffing for our scarecrow.

Hip+Hop were just as excited! The lawn had just been mowed, and before Old Bramble had, had a chance to rake up the grass, they rushed off to gather it up in piles with their fluffy tails!

Bizzie, Bossy and Flossy went over to Mrs Brambles to see if she had any old clothes that Old Bramble didn't need anymore. "Ooh I'll have a look for you ladies." Off she went upstairs, leaving us all with a glass of cloudy lemonade while we waited.

She returned not long after with an old shirt and some patched up dungarees; these will be just fine.

Meanwhile Doris and Delilah had been flying all over to see if they could see any spare bits of wood lying about; we would need to make a post to put our scarecrow on. They found some broken wood down by the compost heap and Pippa the dog was more than happy to pull it across to the lawn, where everyone was gathering.

So...we had wood to make a post. Bluebell was fetching the straw and we had the shirt and dungarees from Mrs Bramble and not to forget all the grass Hip+ Hop had collected, that could be used to give our scarecrow a big fat tummy!

Miss Agatha and Lady Lilliana got to stitching the cuffs and bottoms, so Miss Polly and Miss Dolly could start stuffing them with the straw and grass.

Old Bramble brought his tool box and he fixed up the wood plants to make a good, sturdy post so we could fix him on. "Who says he's a boy scarecrow," said Fleur.

Bizzie, Bossy and Flossy all laughed together and said, "Because boys are scarier!"

Old Bramble said, "What about the head?"

Bluebell said that she'd seen some leftover turnips in the barn when she'd been getting the straw, and took Monsieur Bertie and Percival to go and find the biggest one.

There was just one thing missing—a hat, but nobody had one!
Ms Agnes brought out refreshments for us all and chocolate cookies!
Yummy! "We've no hat. Ms Agnes," said Hip+ Hop.
"Mmm let me think—Fleur do we still have the bonnet left over from the
Easter bonnet parade?"
"Yes of course," said Fleur, "why didn't I think of that hat?"
"It's in the bits n bobs box at the butterfly farm." Not wasting any time,
Doris and Delilah flew over to fetch it.
Everything was starting to come together, Old Bramble fixed the
scarecrow on his post and Bertie and Percival brought back the finest,
biggest turnip for his head. We were just waiting for the Easter bonnet.
"Well done everyone for their help...we have the best scarecrow...do you
want to see him?"

Oh No. Not
My Strawberry Jam!

It was summer and the weather had been very kind to us; it was lovely
and hot which was always better for the fruit and veg. We were going to
have a busy day as all the strawberries needed picking. Some we sold in
Punnett's in the farm shop and the rest we used for Mrs Brambles award
winning Jam! Of course, we were allowed to eat as many as we could
while we picked them.

The only person that couldn't eat them was me—'Monsieur Bertie'. I like
them—but they don't like me; it's a good job. I'm used to running because
that's what they made me do—run all the way to the toilet...If you know
what I mean!!! Whenever we sold a jar of jam, we always asked the
person to return it; it's a good way to recycle.

Mrs Bramble brought out her cloudy lemonade to drink because it was
very hot underneath the day time sun, which went down a treat. Every
strawberry had been picked and there was more than enough. Not all
the jars were returned with their lids so it was Fleur, Doris and Delilah's
job to cut out patches of pretty material to cover them with pretty ribbon
wrapped around them. It was up to Hip+ Hop to stick the labels on;
normally it was the job of Bizzie, Bossy and Flossy, but they had taken a
beach holiday, with some of Flossy's relatives.

Mrs Bramble and Ms Agnes were busy boiling the sugar and Jam, making it taste delicious; the smell was out of this world. They stayed up all through the night to get it finished, so in the morning they baked fresh bread and scones to have with the jam—DELICIOUS! When it had cooled just a little, Old Bramble poured it out into the clean jars, with the lids put on and tied with ribbon and put on a little cart pulled up to the Old barn, where they would be stored.

A couple of days later Old Bramble and Pippa had gone up to the old barn to fetch the wheelbarrow. As he opened the door, there was such a clatter and smashing, something red, hairy and sticky bumped into him and headed straight out of the barn! Just at that moment, in walked Mrs Bramble, "Oh no not my jam, my strawberry jam!"

There was jam everywhere; lids, broken jars...and as she looked closely a sticky, line of footprints...or should I say 'hoof prints', leading right out of the barn! Hip+ Hop had heard the commotion and come to see what was going on.

They all followed the sticky prints all across the bare strawberry patch and they disappeared into the potting shed behind the compost heap.

Mrs Bramble was furious as she swung open the door...she couldn't believe her eyes...a baby red goat! Only red because it was covered in her red strawberry jam! He was enjoying licking the sweet, tasty jam from his fur. "Oh look," Mrs Brambles heart melted.

"Hi I'm 'Ambrose'!" He's one of our new additions to the family. So, we had no jam, but that didn't matter because we had a
new friend—'AMBROSE!'

Where Have All the Carrots Gone!

For each season we have a cake competition; for spring there is usually a light sponge, maybe jam and buttercream. Summer, some kind of fruit sponge. Autumn is something a bit warmer and spicy like apple or ginger and Christmas can be anything, fruit, chocolate coffee or toffee cake. Mrs Bramble always does a 'very fine' chocolate cake, with a chocolate buttercream, chocolate buttons and chocolate sprinkles!

It was the first time Fleur was entering a cake competition. She had decided to make a lovely carrot cake. "Carrot cake," I said, "it's a vegetable not to be put into a cake." Little Percival thought the world of Fleur.

"Oh. I think it will be delightful. Fleur will make it beautiful."

"I'd be careful."

I laughed, "Next year she might decide to put you into a cake; a pea green cake."

Percival wasn't amused and rolled off to see if he could be of any help to Fleur.

"Hi Percival, we are going with Fleur to collect the carrots for the cake, are you coming too?" Of course, he was; Percival wouldn't miss a chance of spending time with Fleur. She was so beautiful, always looked so pretty and moved like a delicate butterfly.

When we got across to the veggie patch, Old Bramble was there scratching his head. "What's wrong Bramble?"
"They're all gone...the carrots are all gone!" He was right. There wasn't a single carrot left! Nobody could understand.
"What am I going to do now?" said Fleur. "That was the only cake I wanted to make." Looking so sad, she turned around and went back towards the butterfly farm, with Doris and Delilah following right behind her. It broke Percival's little heart, to see Fleur like that, so disappointed; he was determined to find out where they had all gone.

I had just joined the conversation. I had been sprinting across the upper meadow. "I bet it has something to do with them naughty bunnies; they'll eat carrots until they sprout out of their ears!" Maybe he was right! Hip+Hop hadn't been around for days; maybe this was the reason, because they would certainly get into trouble.

Percival found them with Bluebell up in the meadow, chasing a ball around. "Is it true, that you've stolen all the carrots that Fleur was going to use for her cake?" Percival said.

"What's this?" asked Bluebell and both Hip+Hop looked up
with astonishment
"We haven't taken any carrots; how could you think we could even do
something like that to Fleur, knowing she would be needing them?" and off
they hopped, looking back with such disappointment that I could even ask
such a question. Now I'd gotten them all upset too! Even Bluebell, kicked
the ball over the wall and walked off towards the barn. Mrs Bramble was
taking some ham and jam sandwiches for Old Bramble's lunch. Pippa
sprinted past her with a big stick in her mouth.
"Hello husband," she said, "I've brought your lunch, your favourite."

I'm going to fetch some more cream from the farm shop. I need it to make my filling for my cake, ready for tomorrow."

She had called in to say 'Hello' to Miss Agatha and Lady Lilliana on her way to get the cream and they were telling her all about the missing carrots! When she got the cream she needed, she was just going around the corner...when Pippa bounced past her, nearly knocking her over...Miss Bramble dropped the cream all over herself and all over the floor! Doris and Delilah were flying over and saw what happened; they chased after Pippa to see what the rush was. She ran past the cottage, over the lawn, through the strawberry patch and over to where the fruit trees grow. Doris and Delilah didn't let her out of their sight for one moment. As they flew closer and hid in the trees, they could see Pippa digging and hiding something as she dug down, all they could see was a sheet of 'orange'.

"Ohh my goodness, there's all the carrots! Pippa's been taking them and hiding them! Quick we must let everyone know."

Old Bramble got his wheelbarrow. "Come on you lot; we have no time to waste getting those carrots if 'Fleur' is going to be making that cake!"

Even hip+hop came back to help after Percival had blamed them! The carrots were washed, grated and ready to go into 'Fleur's cake.

"I haven't got much time," said Fleur.

"It's okay," said Old Bramble. "We are all here to help you," and so they did. By the time they had finished, 'it was exquisite'; the finest you've ever seen.

Third place goes to Mary Rose!

Second place goes to Mrs Bramble and in First place—'Fleur' of Bluebell farm!

Can you guess who had the first slice...?

Yes, Pippa!

CPSIA information can be obtained
at www.ICGtesting.com
Printed in the USA
LVHW071550040521
686459LV00025B/1458